Greek Myths

Retold from the classic originals
by Diane Namm

Illustrated by Eric Freeberg

STERLING

New York / London
www.sterlingpublishing.com/kids

STERLING and the distinctive Sterling logo
are registered trademarks of Sterling Publishing Co., Inc.

Library of Congress Cataloging-in-Publication Data

Namm, Diane.
 Greek myths / retold from the classic originals by Diane Namm ; illustrated by
Eric Freeberg.
     p. cm. — (Classic starts)
  ISBN 978-1-4027-7312-9
  1. Mythology, Greek—Juvenile literature. I. Freeberg, Eric. II. Title.
  BL783.N36 2011
  398.20938—dc22

                                                                    2010039803

Lot#:
2 4 6 8 10 9 7 5 3
08/11
Published by Sterling Publishing Co., Inc.
387 Park Avenue South, New York, NY 10016
Text © 2011 by Diane Namm
Illustrations © 2011 by Eric Freeberg
Distributed in Canada by Sterling Publishing
$^{c}/_{o}$ Canadian Manda Group, 165 Dufferin Street
Toronto, Ontario, Canada M6K 3H6
Distributed in the United Kingdom by GMC Distribution Services
Castle Place, 166 High Street, Lewes, East Sussex, England BN7 1XU
Distributed in Australia by Capricorn Link (Australia) Pty. Ltd.
P.O. Box 704, Windsor, NSW 2756, Australia

Classic Starts is a trademark of Sterling Publishing Co., Inc.

Printed in China
All rights reserved

Sterling ISBN 978-1-4027-7312-9

For information about custom editions, special sales, premium and
corporate purchases, please contact Sterling Special Sales
Department at 800-805-5489 or specialsales@sterlingpublishing.com.

CONTENTS

ᕲ

Introduction to the Gods

⌒

The Greeks believed that the universe created the gods. Before there were gods, there was Heaven and Earth. Father Sky and Mother Earth were the first parents.

The children of GAEA, Mother Earth, and OURANOS, Father Sky, were not quite human. In fact, they were unlike any form of creature known to people. They were giant monsters with terrible, forceful energy. They had the overwhelming strength of an earthquake, a hurricane, and a volcano combined.

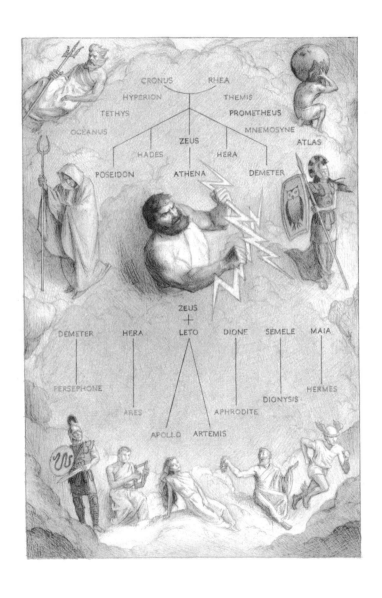

The TITANS were also the children of Heaven and Earth. The Titans were known as the Elder Gods. They ruled the universe for many ages. The Titans were enormous in size and had incredible strength.

CRONUS was the most important Titan. He ruled over all the others. Then his son ZEUS overthrew him and stole the power of the universe from him. Some other important Titans were OCEANUS and his wife, TETHYS; HYPERION, the father of the sun, moon, and dawn; MNEMOSYNE, the goddess of memory; THEMIS, the goddess of justice; ATLAS, who held the world on his shoulders; and PROMETHEUS, who gave fire to humans, saving them from dying out.

ZEUS became the king of the gods. In the beginning, Zeus and his brothers divided up which areas they would rule. Zeus became the supreme ruler. He was the Lord of the Sky, the

Rain-god, and the Cloud-gatherer. He could throw down a terrible thunderbolt whenever he was angry. Zeus's power was greater than that of all the other gods combined. He could appear in many shapes and forms. He often fooled mortals into thinking he was something he was not. Sometimes he was even invisible. But the rustling of oak leaves was one way to know that Zeus was there.

HERA was Zeus's wife. She was the protector of marriage and married women. But in most stories, Hera is described as jealous and mean. She liked to punish humans even if they had done nothing wrong. Also, Hera never forgot if someone did something bad to her. She always wanted vengeance and was usually unstoppable.

POSEIDON was the ruler of the sea. He was Zeus's brother and was second to him in power and importance. Poseidon had a splendid palace beneath the sea. But he was most often found on Mount Olympus. Both storm and calm were controlled by Poseidon. When he drove his golden chariot over the water, the waves became still. Peace followed his smooth-rolling wheels. Yet Poseidon was also known as the Earth-shaker. He would use his trident, a three-pronged spear, to shake up the sea and earth. Poseidon, the god of the sea, was very important to the Greeks, since many of them were sailors.

HADES was also Zeus's brother. He ruled the underworld and the dead. His other names were King of the Dead and God of Wealth. He was the god of wealth because precious metals, like gold and silver, are found beneath the earth. Hades hardly ever left his dark underworld to visit Mount Olympus or Earth. No one really wanted him to visit, either. He wasn't an evil god, but he was still quite terrible.

His wife was PERSEPHONE, queen of the lower world. Persephone's mother was DEMETER, goddess of the corn, summertime, and harvest.

ATHENA was Zeus's daughter. She had no mother. Zeus's favorite child, Athena sprang from his head. She came out fully grown and dressed in full armor as a fierce battle-goddess. She had no pity for her enemies. As Zeus's favorite, she got to carry his terrible thunderbolt weapon. But Athena was also considered the goddess of the city. City life, handicrafts, and farming were under her care. She also represented reason, wisdom, and purity.

APOLLO was the son of Zeus and LETO, the invisible goddess. His other names were Lord of the Silver Bow, the Archer-god, and the Healer. He was the god who first taught mortals how to heal. Apollo was filled with goodness. As the god of the sun, he had no darkness in him at all. He was also known as the god of truth.

ARTEMIS was Apollo's twin sister. As the Lady of Wild Things, she was a hunter to the gods. She was also the protector of children. Just as Apollo was the sun, Artemis was the moon.

APHRODITE was the goddess of love and beauty. She was born from the foam of the sea. Wherever Aphrodite went, beauty followed. She was irresistible to all whom she met. Winds and storm clouds let her pass easily. Sweet flowers begged to be under her foot. The waves of the sea laughed when she was among them. Without her, there would be no joy anywhere. Aphrodite was a soft and gentle goddess. None of the other gods would ever cause her harm.

HERMES was a son of Zeus. He moved swiftly and gracefully everywhere he went. There were wings on his hat and his magic wand. He also wore winged sandals. These wings helped him move freely between the world of gods and the world of humans. For this reason, Hermes was

Zeus's messenger. He also led souls down to their last home in the underworld, Hades. Of all the gods, Hermes was the cleverest.

DIONYSUS was the god of merriment and fun. Sometimes he brought joy and laughter to the people. But sometimes he did cruel and heartless things. Under his influence, courage blossomed in people's hearts. He could move them to do wonderful, brave, and artful things. He made humans feel as if they, too, could be like the gods. Dionysus was much loved by people. He was very important to them.

The GRACES were a group of lovely sisters. Their names were Aglaia (Splendor), Euphrosyne (Mirth), and Thalia (Good Cheer). They were the daughters of Zeus and Eurynome, who was the daughter of Oceanus the Titan. The Graces were elegant and beautiful. They delighted both the gods and mortals. Together with the Muses, they were considered the queens of song. No celebration was complete without them.

The MUSES were nine sisters. They were the daughters of Zeus and Mnemosyne. Clio was the muse of history. Urania was muse of astronomy. Melpomene was the muse of tragedy and Thalia was the muse of comedy. Terpsichore was the muse of dance. Calliope was the muse of classic poetry and Erato was the muse of love poetry. Polyhymnia was the muse of songs to the gods. Euterpe was the muse of lyric poetry. When the nine sisters visited gods or mortals, all troubles would disappear. The Muses were good friends of Apollo and the Graces. Anyone favored by the Muses was considered godly, even if he wasn't a god.

CHAPTER 1

War Among the Gods

⌒

The Greeks have a myth of what existed long before their gods. They thought there was only unbroken darkness and silence. Chaos, which was nothingness and confusion, ruled over Night. Night covered everything above the ground and also ruled over Erebus, the underworld. There was nothing else in the whole universe. All was black, empty, silent, and endless.

Then, from somewhere unknown, Love flooded the universe. It brought Light and Day with it. The sky turned blue in the Light. It filled with stars in the Night. Love brought wind, rain, thunder, and lightning. Then two strange, gigantic beings formed. They were known as Gaea, Mother Earth, and Ouranos, Father Sky. These two created stranger and even more gigantic monsters.

The first type of monster had no name. Each one had fifty heads and one hundred hands. They had the strength of an earthquake, the temper of a hurricane, and the breath of a volcano. These beasts roamed the world. They lifted mountains and scooped out seas. After a while, Ouranos sent them away to the underworld. He could not stand the sight of them.

The second kind of monsters was the Cyclopes. They each had one enormous eye in the middle of their foreheads. Ouranos did not like the Cyclopes. But he allowed them to roam free as long as they kept out of his way.

Then a third type of monster was created.

They were called Titans. These creatures were very strong and smart. A creature named Cronus was the smartest and strongest Titan.

Cronus had many sons and daughters with his wife, Rhea. Cronus was all-powerful, but there was one thing he was very afraid of. It had been said that one day, one of his sons would overpower him. So every time a son was born to him, Cronus put the boy in prison. Rhea begged him not to do this. He didn't listen to her.

When their sixth son was born, Rhea tricked Cronus. She did not tell her husband that she had given birth. Then she sent her son, named Zeus, to live secretly on a nearby island.

Zeus grew up and became a mighty god himself. One day he visited Gaea, his grandmother. She told him about his five brothers who were imprisoned by his father, Cronus.

Zeus became very angry at his father. Gaea

told Zeus where to find Cronus. Zeus went to him at once and demanded that Cronus free his brothers. At first, Cronus refused. But Gaea joined forces with Zeus. Then Cronus had no choice but to free Zeus's brothers.

Not long after, Zeus gathered together his brothers and sisters.

"We must rise up against Cronus and the other Titans," Zeus told them. "They are cruel. They don't understand how the world should be," he added. "But I do."

"How do we do it?" asked one of his brothers.

"Cronus is all-powerful," added one of his sisters.

Zeus needed some advice. So he went to Prometheus and Atlas, two of Cronus's Titan brothers. They also did not like the way that Cronus ruled.

"How can I defeat Cronus?" Zeus asked the two Titans.

"Release the no-name, hundred-handed, fifty-headed monsters from the underworld," Prometheus said. "They have the power of thunder, lightning, earthquake, and volcano. Atlas, my brother, am I right?"

But Atlas said, "I want no part of a war against Cronus." He walked away.

"You will regret your choice one day," Zeus called after him.

"Do what I say and you will defeat Cronus," Prometheus told Zeus.

So Zeus did just that. He released the unnamed, hundred-handed, fifty-headed beast from the underworld.

Zeus—along with his brothers, his sisters, and the monsters—fought a long, dreadful war against the Titans.

The sea crashed against the shores. The earth trembled. The mountains shook. Thunder rumbled. Lightning struck fiercely. The air was filled with fire. The world was whipped into a terrible frenzy.

Zeus took the power of thunder and lightning for himself. He used it, without mercy, against Cronus and the Titans. Zeus was victorious.

Cronus and the other Titans were cast into the underworld. There they would live forever in chains. Zeus came up with a special punishment for Atlas. For refusing to help, Atlas was sent by the king of the gods to the place in the world where Night met Day. He was forced to hold up the world on his shoulders forever.

As a reward for Prometheus's help, Zeus gave him and his brother Epimetheus a special honor. They were to create humans and all the animals on Earth. The brothers also were to decide what each creatures' special gifts would be.

Zeus, his brothers, and his sisters became the only ruler-gods of the world. They chose the

most perfect place on Earth to live—Mount Olympus. It was the highest point on Earth, and the closest to Heaven. It never rained, and no cold winds blew there. The sun always shone down on the gods when they were on Mount Olympus.

Zeus and the gods led delightful lives. Apollo, god of the sun, played beautiful songs on his harp. The Muses sang for them. The Graces danced for them. The gods ate ambrosia and drank nectar, the godliest of food and drink. They never knew pain or grief. The gods were known as the immortal Olympians, and they ruled over the entire world.

CHAPTER 2

Demeter and Persephone

Most of the gods lived happily on Mount Olympus. One goddess did not. Her name was Demeter. She was the goddess of the corn, summertime, and harvest. When Demeter was happy, the world was filled with golden light. The stalks in the cornfields grew thick and tall. Everyone in the world had enough to eat.

But every year after the corn harvest, Demeter became sad. A frost would blanket the fields. The ground became hard and frozen. Every bit of life was squeezed out of the earth.

This is why it happened.

Demeter had a daughter. Her name was Persephone, the maiden of spring. Throughout the world, she was known as the most beautiful girl. A golden glow of sunlight surrounded her. Persephone's hair was the pale yellow color of freshly cut corn. Her cheeks were rosy pink. Her voice was like a bird's song. Persephone's musical laughter could be heard everywhere. Her laughter even reached down to where Hades ruled as lord of the underworld.

I wish Persephone was my wife. If she lived here with me, she would bring light and music to this lonely, terrible place, Hades thought.

But he knew that Demeter would never allow Persephone to marry him. He had asked the goddess once before and was refused. So he came up with a plan. Hades had to wait for just the right moment. Then he would take Persephone as his bride.

One day, Persephone was out with her friends in the meadow. A perfect flower had caught her eye, and she wandered far away. Persephone wanted to give the flower to Demeter to put in her hair.

Suddenly the earth beneath Persephone's feet began to shake. The ground cracked in half at her feet. Hades burst up from the underworld. He rode a dark chariot drawn by four coal-black horses. He grabbed Persephone by the hand. Before she could call out, he pulled her close to him. Hades raced the chariot back to the underworld. Persephone wept and shouted for her mother.

Persephone's cries echoed throughout the world. Her sobs were heard from the highest hills to the deepest parts of the sea. Demeter heard Persephone weeping. She flew like a bird over land and sea to find her daughter.

"Where is Persephone?" she asked everyone

she met. "Have you seen her? Where has she gone?" No one would tell Demeter what had happened. The truth was just too terrible.

Demeter searched for Persephone for nine days. She refused to eat or drink. At last Demeter went to Mount Olympus. She wanted to speak with Apollo, the sun god. He saw everything and would know where her daughter was. Apollo told her everything.

"Persephone is down in the underworld. She will live there among the shadows forever," he said to her.

Demeter's heart filled with sorrow. She flew away from Mount Olympus.

For one whole year, Demeter grieved for Persephone. She disguised herself as a human and wandered the Earth. Without her daughter, there was no happiness for Demeter. The goddess then decided there would be no spring, summer, or harvest. That year was dreadful and cruel for humankind all over Earth. Nothing grew anywhere. Everyone nearly died of hunger.

Zeus sent the gods from Mount Olympus to plead with Demeter. They asked her to stop punishing the world with her sorrow. They begged her to allow the fruits and vegetables to grow again.

But Demeter said she would not do it. The world would remain this way until she could see Persephone again. Finally, Zeus sent Hermes to the underworld with a message to Hades: "Return Persephone to Demeter."

When Hermes arrived, he found Persephone curled up in a dark corner. She was small and thin. Since being kidnapped to the underworld she had eaten nothing. She knew not to eat anything while she was there. If she did, she would never be able to return to the Earth and to her mother.

Persephone heard Hermes's message to Hades. She sprang up joyfully, and was eager to leave. Hades knew he had to obey Zeus. But there was one thing he could do to make Persephone return to him.

"Dear Persephone, think kindly of me when you return to Earth. Please, take this pomegranate to eat on your way."

Hades slipped the pomegranate into the hand of Persephone. Then he ordered his chariot to return both Hermes and Persephone to the world above.

Persephone forgot that she wasn't supposed to eat anything from the underworld. She was too excited, and the fruit looked delicious. Without thinking, she ate the pomegranate seeds Hades had given her.

The chariot returned Persephone to her mother.

When Demeter saw Persephone, she ran to meet her. Persephone jumped into her mother's arms. They held each other tight.

But then a message arrived from Zeus.

"Persephone has eaten three pomegranate seeds from the underworld. Therefore, she must return to Hades for three months of every year. These are the laws," Zeus told her.

Persephone sobbed. Demeter hugged her daughter closer. But they both knew that they could not disobey. This was the law of the underworld.

So now for three months each year, Persephone returns to her husband, Hades, ruler of the underworld. For those three months, Demeter grieves. The world turns cold and bitter. The ground freezes and nothing can grow. Winter takes over the land.

CHAPTER 3

Heracles

～

Heracles was the strongest man who ever lived. His father was the god Zeus and his mother was a human. When he was just a baby, two poisonous snakes slithered into Heracles's crib. But was he scared? Heracles was not.

Instead, he grabbed each snake with a chubby fist. He tossed them out the window. Then he laughed and giggled in his crib.

Everyone knew that Heracles was bound for great things. And everyone loved him, except for Hera, queen of the gods.

When Heracles was a grown man, Hera decided to throw trouble his way. She convinced her cousin King Eurystheus to send Heracles on a quest to complete impossible tasks. Heracles would have to prove that he was the strongest man in the world. He could not turn the king down. His pride was too great. Heracles agreed to the quest. Hera's hope was that Heracles would not be able to complete the tasks.

"First, you must kill the lion of Nemea. It is a beast that no weapons can wound," the king told Heracles.

"As you wish, King," Heracles said.

Heracles hunted down the great lion. He strangled the beast with his bare hands. Then he returned to the kingdom.

"What is my next task?" asked Heracles.

"You must kill the nine-headed Hydra," said the king.

"As you wish, King," said Heracles.

Killing the Hydra was a most difficult job. It was also very dangerous. One of the Hydra's heads was immortal and could never die. But the other eight heads were worse. If one was chopped off, two more grew back in its place! Each of its nine mouths spewed deadly, poisonous breath.

But Heracles set out for the adventure anyway. His strength and smarts were endless. Along the journey, Heracles figured out a way to kill the nine-headed Hydra.

After a long and harsh voyage to the lake of Lerna, Heracles met the terrible Hydra. True to legend, it breathed terrible poison. Its nine heads darted and snapped at Heracles. But the strongest man alive was prepared. Heracles cut off each of the Hydra's nine heads with a mighty sword. He buried the immortal head under the earth and covered it with a heavy rock. Then he sealed each headless neck with a hot iron poker. This prevented the Hydra from growing any heads back.

When Heracles returned to the king, he asked, "Have I proven myself worthy yet?"

"No. Not yet. Next you must tame the wild white deer with golden horns. Bring her to me. She lives in the forest of Artemis, the goddess of hunting," the king demanded.

It took Heracles a year to find the white deer. It ran faster than any other creature. This made it almost impossible to capture. But of course, Heracles was able to do it. Under his hand, the wild deer became meek. As requested, he brought the deer back to the king.

"Here is your white deer," Heracles said to the king. "I have tamed it. It is gentle as can be."

"Now bring me the great boar from Mount Erymanthos," the king commanded.

Heracles went out to perform this task. He went up to the mountain and searched for the beast. Once he found the boar, Heracles chased it up the mountain. He was able to drive the beast into the deep snow at the top of the mountain. There he trapped the creature and brought it back to the king.

But the king was not done giving Heracles missions. Hera made the king continue Heracles's quest. There were to be twelve tasks in all. Each one was equally difficult, or humiliating, or painful. Each time Heracles set out to complete a task, he was successful.

The last part of the quest was the worst of all.

"Bring me Cerberus, the three-headed dog from Hades. I want him brought to me alive. Then you will have finally proven yourself to be the strongest man in the world," the king said.

Heracles bravely went down into the underworld. No mortal ever dared to go there. The trip was horrible. It was difficult for a person to enter and exit the underworld alive. The gods

Athena and Hermes helped Heracles travel safely.

When Heracles arrived at the entrance to Hades's lair, he could barely see anything. But he heard a growl in the darkness. It sounded like three growls in one.

This must be Cerberus, Heracles thought. He began to speak to the god of the underworld. He knew that Hades would be standing close to his three-headed dog.

"Hades, hear me. I am Heracles, sent by King Eurystheus. I must bring him your dog, Cerberus, in order to be released from my horrible quest. Will you allow it?" Heracles called into the darkness.

"You may take my Cerberus—but only if you can take him without harming him. You may use no weapons to capture him," Hades warned.

Heracles agreed.

Cerberus jumped at him. Man and dog

wrestled for hours. The dog's three sets of vicious teeth snapped at him from every direction. Heracles used all his strength to hold down the beast. At last Cerberus became too tired and stopped fighting. All three of the dog's heads were gasping for air. Heracles had overcome the beast and was champion of the fight. He lifted Cerberus and returned to the king's palace.

"I have brought you Cerberus, the three-headed dog of Hades," Heracles exclaimed to the king. He laid the dog at the king's feet and sat down beside it, exhausted. The king couldn't believe that Heracles had completed each task.

"You have performed all twelve tasks. I have nothing more to ask. You have nothing more to prove, to me or to anyone," the king told him. "You will forever be known as Heracles, the strongest man on Earth."

CHAPTER 4

Pandora

⌒

From high up on Mount Olympus, the gods liked to play tricks on the humans below.

There was once a shy young woman. She had long, silky hair and large, sky-blue eyes. She was sweet and lovely, and had beauty that shone like the sun. Since she had been blessed with these good qualities, she was called Pandora. Her name means "the gift of all."

One day, Zeus saw her through the mist that separated Mount Olympus from the Earth.

"Pandora is the most perfect of all women," the god said.

"She is no better or worse than any other mortal woman," said Hera, Zeus's jealous wife.

"She is perfection," Zeus declared.

"I say she is just like any mortal woman," Hera insisted. "And I shall prove it."

"What are you going to do?" Zeus asked.

"I shall give her this beautiful box," Hera said. "I will fill it with all the troubles that a mortal can have: sorrow, mischief, sickness, sadness, and death. When we give it to her, we will tell her not to open it. If she is as perfect as you say, then she will not be tempted. And mortals will have nothing to fear, for all their troubles will remain in the box."

"I will throw in hope with the evils you've included," Zeus said. Hera and Zeus both went down from Mount Olympus. They gave Pandora the magnificent box and warned her not to open it. Then Hera and Zeus returned to Mount Olympus to see what Pandora would do.

Day after day, Pandora gazed at the lovely box. Its ruby-red stones sparkled in the moonlight. Its gold cover twinkled in the sunlight. It was beautiful. She should have been happy with it just as it was. But she wanted to know what was inside. Pandora could think of nothing else.

Every day, Pandora walked to the box and reached for its lid. Then she'd pull her hand away before she could open it.

"See," said Zeus. "I told you Pandora was perfect. She will not open it because we told her not to."

"We shall see," Hera said.

Many weeks went by. Pandora still gazed at the box every day. One day, she could stand it no longer. She had to know what was inside.

Pandora knelt before the box. Slowly, and with great delight, she lifted the heavy lid just a crack. She peeked inside.

At once a terrible wind blew the lid wide open. The air was filled with a tornado of shrieks, whistles, moans, and cries. Sorrow, mischief, sickness, sadness, and death all escaped from the box Pandora had opened.

In terror, Pandora clapped the lid down. But it was too late. All the evils that would trouble humankind forever flew out of Pandora's box that day. Everything escaped but one thing— hope. The hope that Zeus had put into the box remained. It was the only good thing the box contained. To this day hope is humankind's only comfort in times of trouble.

"Now what do you say?" Hera asked Zeus. They watched the disaster that Pandora had let loose upon the world. Zeus took a sip of nectar and a bite of ambrosia.

"I'm waiting . . . ," Hera said.

"You were right and I was wrong," Zeus told her with a sigh. "But we shall see what happens the next time we play a trick on the mortals."

"Yes. We shall see, indeed," Hera said with a satisfied smile.

CHAPTER 5

Echo and Narcissus

〜

Once there was a handsome young man named Narcissus. His hair was black as coal. His eyes sparkled with fire. His face was good-looking, and his body was strong. Everywhere he went, young women fainted at the sight of him. Narcissus cared for none of them. His heart was as cold as ice and he was only interested in himself. He paid no attention to anyone he met.

There was one young woman who lived in the forest near Narcissus. Her name was Echo. She was a beautiful, happy young woman. She always laughed and chattered with her many friends. Echo was a favorite of Artemis, the goddess of the woods and wild creatures. But she was not a favorite of Hera. Hera was always jealous of beautiful mortal girls. One day, she heard Echo's happy chatter and became very angry. In a jealous fit of rage, Hera decided to punish Echo.

"You may never use your tongue again except to repeat what has been said to you. You will always have the last word," Hera told Echo, "but you will have no power to speak first."

Hera went back to Mount Olympus, satisfied.

Poor Echo. She didn't understand why Hera wanted to punish her. Even worse, at that moment Narcissus walked past her. Like all the other young maidens, Echo fell hopelessly in love with him. She followed Narcissus, but she could not speak to him. How would she ever be able to get him to notice her?

One day, it seemed her chance had come. Echo had seen Narcissus while he was sitting by a lake. She shyly hung back among the trees. But Narcissus heard a rustling in the leaves.

"Is anyone here?" he called out.

"Here . . . Here!" Echo called back with joy.

"Come!" Narcissus shouted into the trees where the voice had come from.

"Come!" Echo replied. She stepped from behind the trees. Her arms were open wide, and she had a loving look in her eyes.

"Do you mock me?" Narcissus asked angrily. "I would rather die than do what you want." Then he turned and walked away.

Echo was crushed. And all she could say back to him was "Do what you want." But Narcissus was gone.

Artemis heard what had happened to Echo. She complained to the great goddess Nemesis, the righter of wrongs.

"We shall have our revenge on this cruel, selfish Narcissus," Nemesis told Artemis.

"What will you do?" Artemis wanted to know.

"I will put a spell on him to make him fall in love with the first thing he sees," Nemesis said.

Later that day, Narcissus bent over a clear pond for a drink. Nemesis cast her spell at that moment. Narcissus saw his own reflection. In that instant, he fell in love with it. He reached out to touch the face he saw mirrored in the water.

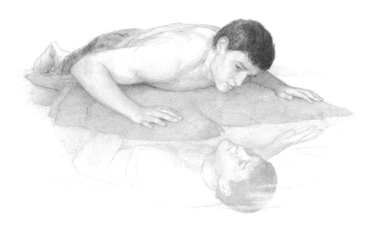

But it disappeared. Only when he remained still could he gaze into the lovely creature's eyes.

"Ah, me!" Narcissus said. "It is torture to love someone I can never have!"

So deep was his love that he refused to leave the pond, not even to eat or drink. Instead, he leaned over the pond's edge. His eyes were fixed, staring into his own reflected face.

Echo was nearby, but she could do nothing to save him. Narcissus slowly wasted away. When the last bit of life was leaving him, Narcissus called out, "Farewell!" to the image in the water.

All Echo could do was also call out, "Farewell!" She was so sad that she took shelter in a lonely cave. She lives there to this day. Only her voice remains. Her body has wasted away with longing for her poor Narcissus.

As for Narcissus, the creatures of the wood, who also admired his beauty, took pity on him. They wished him to be remembered well. In the spot where he had last looked upon his reflection, they planted a new and lovely flower. From the time it began to bloom it was known as the "Narcissus" flower.

CHAPTER 6

Orpheus and Eurydice

The gods on Mount Olympus made heavenly and beautiful music. All who heard it were enchanted. There was one mortal who could make music as beautiful as the gods. His name was Orpheus.

Orpheus was the son of one of the Muses. She gave him the gift of music. She hoped it would keep him safe when she could not be with him.

When Orpheus played his harp and sang, there was no limit to his power. No one and nothing could resist him. If mortals argued in front of him, Orpheus would play his harp tenderly and soothingly. The fiercest fighters would grow calm and forget their anger. The power of his song was so great that he could move rocks on a hillside. He could even change the direction in which a river flowed.

One day, Orpheus met Eurydice. She was one of the loveliest maidens in the land. He fell in love with her instantly. In order to make her fall in love with him, he played his music for her. His song was so sweet that she did fall in love with him. They were married the very next day.

Right after the wedding, Eurydice and Orpheus crossed the meadow to their new home. On the way, she was bitten by a snake in the grass. Eurydice died that night.

Orpheus was overcome with sadness. He decided he could not live without his wife. So Orpheus journeyed into the underworld. He went to bring his Eurydice back.

As Orpheus went deeper and deeper into the underworld, he played his harp and sang his sweet song. His music charmed all below into stillness. Cerberus, the mean three-headed dog, whimpered like a puppy. The Furies, the bitter goddesses of the underworld, wept at the sad and sweet song. Even Hades's heart melted at the sound of Orpheus's voice. Each of them stood as still as a statue when they heard Orpheus's song. They could not make a move to harm him.

Orpheus saw Eurydice walking down into the darkest depths of the underworld. He called out to her, but she could not answer. She was already half ghost and unable to speak.

Orpheus begged Hades to allow him to return above the ground with Eurydice. Hades gave in.

"I will allow her to return with you—on one condition," Hades told him.

"Anything," Orpheus agreed.

"She will follow you up to Earth. I promise. But you may not turn your head to look back at her until you have completely left the underworld," Hades warned. Orpheus agreed.

So Orpheus and Eurydice passed through the great doors of Hades. They took the path that would bring them out of the underworld. They climbed up.

Orpheus knew that Eurydice had to be right behind him. He longed to glance over his shoulder just once to make sure. But he remembered Hades's words and did not.

They were almost out of the underworld. The blackness was turning gray. They were able to see the light of the sun. Finally, they were back on Earth. Orpheus stepped out joyfully into the sunlight. Then he turned to Eurydice. But he turned too soon!

Eurydice was still in the cavern below. She had not yet stepped back onto Earth. He saw her in the dim gray light. He held out his hand to grab her. But in that instant she was gone!

Orpheus tried to rush after her back into the darkness. But this time he could not. The gods would not allow him to enter the underworld again. A mortal could only enter once while he was still alive. Orpheus had to stay on Earth alone, in despair.

The heartbroken young man spent the rest of his life playing sad songs. They broke the hearts of all who heard them. When Orpheus died, he was laid to rest at the foot of Mount Olympus. To this day, the nightingales sing the sweetest at Mount Olympus—in memory of the song of Orpheus.

CHAPTER 7

Pygmalion and Galatea

There once lived a young sculptor named Pygmalion. He lived on the island of Cyprus. There was no sculptor more talented than he. Pygmalion spent his days hard at work at his art. He had no time for friends or a wife.

"I suppose I shall never find anyone to marry," he said, sadly.

Then one day, Pygmalion came up with a plan. He would create a wife out of marble. She would be the perfect woman. This way, he could sculpt all day and have a companion.

Pygmalion set to work at once. He searched for the most perfect block of marble. He sharpened his sculpting tools to the finest points. Then he began to sculpt.

Pygmalion worked hard. He sculpted with great care. He carved the statue with love. When he was done, it was a fine work of art. Art lovers from all over Cyprus came to view Pygmalion's sculpture.

"Magnificent," said one.

"Amazing," said another.

"Almost life-like," said a third.

But this was not enough for Pygmalion.

He wanted his statue to be the loveliest creation on Earth. Pygmalion continued to work day and night. The statue grew more and more beautiful. No woman ever born and no statue ever made could even come close to its beauty.

When nothing more could be done, Pygmalion stepped back. He gazed into the statue's eyes. At that moment, a strange thing happened. Pygmalion was struck with a feeling he'd never had before. It was love. He had fallen deeply in love with this thing he had made.

Looking at the statue, no one would have thought she was made of stone. Her skin looked warm with life. Her eyes gazed into Pygmalion's soul. Pygmalion was so talented that his own creation looked completely alive, even to him!

"I shall call you Galatea," Pygmalion declared.

Although Pygmalion should have been proud and joyful, he was unhappy instead. No one ever loved as much as Pygmalion loved his statue. He kissed her, as if that could wake her. But her stone lips could not kiss him back. He stroked her long, flowing hair. But the hair did not move beneath his fingers. He held her close in his arms, but she was stiff and unmoving.

Yet Pygmalion would not be troubled. And he could not be taken away from his love. One day,

Pygmalion dressed the statue in rich, expensive clothes.

"Tell me, my love. Do you like the red dress or the blue?" he would ask her.

But the statue did not answer. So Pygmalion pretended that she had.

He brought her special gifts: little birds that sang sweetly, wildflowers with heavenly scents, and sparkling gems in all the colors of the rainbow.

Every evening he tucked her into bed, beneath the softest and warmest blankets.

"Thank you, my dearest," Pygmalion imagined she whispered to him.

Pygmalion did this day after day, and night after night. Until, at last, he could pretend no more. He had to admit that he loved a lifeless thing. Pygmalion was miserable.

That night, Pygmalion found himself in the

deepest despair. He cried out to Aphrodite, the goddess of love, to help him.

"Please help me find a woman as lovely as my sculpture," he asked.

Aphrodite heard Pygmalion's plea. She felt bad for the sad artist who loved his statue.

Pygmalion awoke the next morning. He went to look at his statue on her pedestal. Only this morning, the statue's eyes seemed to follow him wherever he moved. Pygmalion went closer. He reached out to take her beautiful hand. It was warm!

Pygmalion stepped back in surprise. He put his hands upon her shoulders. They became soft under his fingertips.

He leaned in to kiss her gently on the lips. She kissed him back. The statue's entire form softened like wax in the sun.

Pygmalion clasped her wrist and felt a pulse.

He took the statue in his arms. Miraculously, she hugged him back!

"Are you real?" Pygmalion asked. "Or am I dreaming?"

"I'm as real as you, my love," the beautiful woman in his arms answered.

"Will you marry me, Galatea?" Pygmalion asked as he took her hand.

"Yes," she answered simply.

From that day forward, Pygmalion was the happiest man on Earth. He thanked Aphrodite every single day. Aphrodite smiled down on them from Mount Olympus. Another happy ending, thanks to the goddess of love.

CHAPTER 8

Jason and the Golden Fleece

⌒

There once was a young prince named Jason. He was handsome, with blond curly hair that flowed down his back. He was tall and strong. All who met him were impressed.

In Greece, where Jason lived, King Pelias ruled. A great prophet had spoken to the Oracle in Delphi. The Oracle was where people would go when they had a question for the gods. The prophet then told Jason that he was supposed to rule Greece with King Pelias. Jason went to speak with King Pelias about this prediction.

"The Oracle has said that you and I should rule this land together," Jason said.

King Pelias had no interest in sharing his kingdom. Jason was practically still a boy! But he knew that Jason was a favorite of Hera, the queen goddess.

"If that is so," King Pelias replied, "you will have to prove yourself worthy."

"What shall I do?" asked Jason.

"You must go on a quest. Bring back the Golden Fleece that was taken from our kingdom long ago. I am an old man, and too old to go on this quest. But if you succeed, it will bring honor back to our kingdom. Bring back the Golden Fleece from King Aetes of Colchis," King Pelias told him, "and half my kingdom shall be yours."

Jason was delighted by the idea of this great adventure. He announced that he would sail from Greece on the great ship *Argo*. He welcomed men to join him. The best warriors from all over

Greece wanted to come along on his quest. Jason put together a great crew. They were known as the Argonauts.

Hera watched from Mount Olympus and smiled. She sent Jason and the Argonauts flasks of courage potion to drink. This potion would make them fearless against the dangers they would face along the way.

Jason and his fellow Argonauts set sail to search for the Golden Fleece. After traveling for many days, they came to a land called Lemnos. A group of fierce and war-like women lived there.

The women saw Jason at the wheel of the great ship. He looked so strong and brave that the women became gentle and peaceful at once. They offered the Argonauts food and drink. They also offered newly woven clothing to replace the torn clothes they wore. Then they sent the men on their way.

Jason and the Argonauts sailed night and day

in their quest to bring back the Golden Fleece. One night while the ship glided over the dark waters, a terrible smell filled the air. Without warning, frightful creatures attacked the men from the sky. The bird-like things had hooked beaks and sharp claws.

"Harpies!" Jason shouted to his crew. "Take cover!" The men covered their heads and faces with their shields. The Harpies were nasty bird-like creatures that attacked humans. They were created by Zeus to torment an old man named Phineas.

Phineas had been given the gift of truth-telling by Apollo. But he had used his powers to reveal the gods' plans on Earth to too many people. So Zeus sent the Harpies to punish Phineas. Every time Phineas would eat, the Harpies would arrive to steal his food. Then they would leave him with foul smells.

Jason and the Argonauts sailed closer to land.

When they arrived on the shore, they found Phineas, half starved. He begged Jason for help.

"Of course I will help you, old man. What shall I do?" Jason said to Phineas. The old man told Jason that only the sons of the North Wind could free him from the Harpies. Jason went to the sons of the North Wind and asked for help. They were impressed by Jason's confidence and grace. So they agreed to help Phineas.

When the Harpies appeared again, the sons of the North Wind struck the horrible creatures with their swords. The Harpies began to fall from the sky. Iris, the rainbow messenger from Zeus, appeared. She convinced the sons of the North Wind to allow the Harpies to live. Iris promised that the creatures would never trouble Phineas or the Argonauts again.

To thank Jason and the Argonauts for their help, Phineas told Jason the secret to his next obstacle: the Clashing Rocks. These rocks were large boulders that crashed against one another. The sea boiled up around them.

"You must send a dove to fly between the rocks. Notice the speed with which the dove flies. Notice the path that the dove takes. If the dove survives, the *Argo* shall pass safely through. If it does not survive, you will never make it past the rocks. Then you must return home to Greece and give up all hope of finding the Golden Fleece," Phineas warned.

The next morning, the *Argo* reached the Clashing Rocks. Jason did exactly as Phineas had told him. He released a dove. The crew watched carefully as the bird flew swiftly between the rocks. Only the dove's tail feathers were clipped as the rocks rolled back together.

"Let's move!" Jason shouted to the rowers of the *Argo*. They followed the dove's path as quickly as they could.

The rocks opened. The rowers used all their strength. The ship sailed safely through the Clashing Rocks. Only the ornament at the back end of the ship was torn off. The men cheered and the *Argo* continued.

At last, Jason and the Argonauts arrived at their destination: the faraway land of Colchis, kingdom of King Aetes. The men came onto the shore.

Hera knew that King Aetes would not give up the Golden Fleece without a fight. So she covered Jason and his men in a cloud of mist. She hoped to make them invisible. Jason and the Argonauts traveled like this from the shore to the palace of Aetes.

Hera decided she must do more. She went to Aphrodite, the goddess of love, and asked her for a favor. Aphrodite was surprised. She and Hera were not friends. Hera barely even spoke to Aphrodite, much less asked her for favors.

"Please," Hera begged. "You must help Jason get the Golden Fleece. King Aetes's daughter Medea has great magical powers. Make her fall in love with Jason so that she will help him in his quest."

Aphrodite agreed to help. She sent her son Eros down to Earth. He was to wait for just the right moment, then cast a spell of love on Princess Medea.

When Jason and his men arrived at the palace, King Aetes welcomed them. His servants built fires and heated water for their baths. They brought them plates of food to eat. They brought cushions to make the men comfortable.

Princess Medea crept into the dining room. She was curious about her father's guests. The moment she saw Jason, Eros drew his bow and shot his magical arrow deep into her heart. She suddenly fell in love with the handsome young man. Amazed and confused, she stayed to watch and listen.

Jason and the Argonauts were enjoying themselves. They were eating and drinking their fill. Finally, King Aetes sat down with them. He asked who they were and what they wanted.

Jason explained that he had come to Colchis to bring back the Golden Fleece to King Pelias. At that moment King Aetes felt a flash of anger come over him. But he did not want Jason to know he was angry.

"You are very brave to travel all this way to find the Golden Fleece. If you are truly as brave as you seem, you must do what I did to get the Fleece. Then I will let you have it," King Aetes said.

"What must I do?" Jason wanted to know.

"You must get control over my two bulls. They both have feet of bronze, fiery breath, and fierce tempers. Tie them to a yoke and use them to plow a field. Then plant these dragon teeth like corn seeds." King Aetes handed the teeth to Jason. "A crop of armed men will grow. You must cut down these men as they come forward to attack you. I have done all this myself. And I will only give the Golden Fleece to the man who can do what I have done," he added.

For a moment Jason was silent. The task seemed impossible.

"I will do it, sir," Jason replied.

He rose and returned to the ship with the Argonauts for the night. He passed right by Princess Medea on his way out. But he did not notice her. He was thinking about his challenge.

Princess Medea's eyes followed after Jason. After he had left the palace, she imagined she could still see him. She thought about his beauty, his grace, and his wonderful voice. Medea feared what her father had in store for Jason. She guessed that the king wanted Jason to die in his quest for the Golden Fleece. She could not allow that to happen.

Back at the ship, the Argonauts held a meeting. Everyone urged Jason to give up the quest. They all thought it was too dangerous. But Jason would not. Then one of King Aetes's grandsons came aboard. Jason had saved him from death several years back. The king's grandson had not forgotten this. He wanted Jason to succeed in the king's quest. He told Jason of Medea's magic powers.

"There is nothing she can't do," he told Jason. "With Medea on your side, you will be able to capture the bulls and defeat the armed, dragon-teeth men."

Meanwhile, Medea wept in her room.

"How can I care more for a stranger than my own father?" she wondered. "Yet I must protect Jason," she decided. "I cannot live without him."

So Medea decided to use her powers for the

man she loved. She made a magical body potion. When rubbed on, it would protect the wearer and keep him safe for the whole day. Using the potion was like wearing a full suit of armor. Medea sent a message to Jason asking him to meet her in the palace garden.

As soon as he received the message, Jason left to meet Medea. Hera smiled down upon him. She gave him a special glow that night. When Medea saw him in the garden, her love floated toward him. A mist clouded her eyes. She had barely any strength to move. The two stood face-to-face without saying a word. Jason was also enchanted by Medea. Then, stirred by emotion, they began to speak.

"Please, Princess. You must be as kind as you are beautiful. I beg you to help me win the Golden Fleece," Jason said.

Medea did not know how to speak to Jason. She wanted to tell him how she felt all at once.

Instead, silently, Medea took the bottle of potion from her pocket and gave it to him. She would have given him anything.

At last Medea broke her silence.

"Use this charmed potion all over your body. Use it on your weapons, too. It will make you indestructible for a full day. But here is something else you must know. If too many of the armed, dragon-teeth men rush to attack you, throw a stone among them. It will make them turn against one another and fight," she told him.

Medea turned to go, then looked back at him once more.

"When you are safely home, remember Medea," she asked him, "for I will remember you forever."

"Never a night or a day will go by that I don't think of you," Jason promised her. "If you return to Greece with me, I will let nothing come between us."

They left each other. That night, Medea wept in her room. She was in despair over her love for Jason. And she was also in despair over betraying her father.

After Medea left him, Jason tried the potion. When he touched it, he felt an amazing power enter his body. He knew he was ready for King Aetes's test.

The next day, the king and the people of his kingdom were waiting for Jason in the bull field. Jason stepped into the field. The two bulls rushed out, breathing flames of fire. The Argonauts were terrified. But Jason stood his ground against the terrible creatures. He forced both bulls down on their knees and put the yoke on them. Everyone was amazed by his strength and skill.

Jason drove the bulls over the field. He

pressed the plow down firmly into the ground. Then he threw the dragon teeth into the ridges left by the plow. A crop of armed men sprang up from the ground. They came rushing to attack him.

Remembering Medea's words, Jason flung a huge stone into the middle of the group. The warriors turned upon one another and fought.

King Aetes was not pleased. He returned to his palace, fuming. He would never allow Jason to have the Golden Fleece! King Aetes would kill him first.

But Hera was still on Jason's side. She made Medea, dazed with love and misery, decide to leave with Jason. That night, Medea slipped out of the palace. She sped along the dark path to the ship. When she saw Jason, she fell on her knees before him.

"Please, my love. Take me with you! I cannot live without you. We must get the Fleece and leave at once. My father will kill you in the morning," Medea warned Jason. "And once he knows I have helped you, he will kill me, too."

"But where is the Golden Fleece?" Jason asked.

"I can lead you there," Medea told him. "A terrible serpent guards the Fleece. But I can put it to sleep so you will not be harmed."

Jason gently took Medea in his arms. He promised to make her his wife when they returned to Greece.

Medea nearly wept for joy. Then she led Jason to the place where the Fleece was hung. It was on a tree in a hidden wood. The guardian serpent was even more terrible than Medea had described. But she approached it fearlessly. She sang a sweet, magical song to it. The serpent was charmed to sleep.

Swiftly Jason lifted the Golden Fleece from the tree. They hurried back to the *Argo* as dawn was breaking. Jason put his strongest rowers at the oars. With Medea at his side, Jason and his men rowed away from Colchis with all their might.

Jason had his Golden Fleece at last.

CHAPTER 9

Perseus

❦

Perseus was the son of Zeus and a mortal woman, Danae. Perseus lived with his very beautiful mother in a fishing village on a small island.

Polydectes, the ruler of the island, admired Danae's great beauty. He decided he wanted her as his wife. But he did not want Perseus to live with them.

Polydectes knew how much Danae and Perseus loved each other. They would never want to live apart. So he made a plan to get rid of Perseus and marry Danae.

On a nearby island, there lived terrible monsters called Gorgons. They were known for their deadly powers. One day, Polydectes told Perseus about them.

"There are three of them. Each has wings and snakes for hair. They have golden scales that are as hard as armor. Any man who looks at them never breathes again. He turns instantly into stone," Polydectes said. "Medusa is the fiercest of the Gorgons. To tell you the truth," he added to Perseus in a low voice, "I would rather have the head of Medusa than anything else in the world."

The next day, Polydectes announced he would marry Danae. He invited all his friends, including Perseus, to the marriage celebration. All of Polydectes's friends brought great gifts. Perseus sadly had nothing to give. But he was young, proud, and embarrassed. Perseus stood up at the wedding to make an announcement. He did exactly what Polydectes hoped he would do.

"I will give you and my mother the best present of all. I will go and kill Medusa the Gorgon. I will bring back her head as your gift," Perseus promised Polydectes.

"Splendid!" Polydectes said, patting Perseus on the back. "Nothing will make us happier."

Perseus had let his pride and shame take over. His offer was empty. No mortal man could kill Medusa. But two of the most powerful gods, Hermes and Athena, watched over him.

Perseus set sail the next day for the island of the Gorgons. When he arrived, he realized he did not know where the Gorgons lived. No one was able to tell him, either. Perseus searched high and low. Still nobody would direct him to the Gorgons' home.

At last, the gods decided to help him. Perseus

soon met a young man who had a golden wand with wings. He wore a winged hat and winged sandals. It was Hermes, guide and giver of good. Athena had sent him to help Perseus find the Gorgons.

"Before you attack Medusa, you must have the right tools," Hermes explained. "The fairies of the North will know what you need," he added. "But first, we must look for the Gray Women. Only they know where to find the fairies of the North."

Hermes led Perseus through a shadowy forest. All was dim and covered in twilight. No ray of sun or glimmer of moonlight ever shone there. In that gray place lived the three Gray Women. They were old and withered. The women were strange creatures. Among them they had only one eye. They took turns using it. When each woman was done with it, she removed it from her forehead and passed it to the next woman.

"Now, listen carefully, Perseus," Hermes whispered as they came upon the Gray Women. "Stay hidden until you see one of the women take the eye from her forehead. That's when the women cannot see anything. At that moment you must rush forward and grab the eye. Refuse to give it back until they tell you how to reach the fairies of the North."

Perseus and Hermes found the Gray Women at last. In the dim light, the women were in the shape of gray swans. But their heads were human. Beneath their wings they had arms and legs.

Perseus did just as Hermes had instructed him. He stayed back until he saw one of the women take the eye out of her forehead. Before she could give it to her sister, Perseus grabbed the eye from her hand. It took a moment for the women to realize they had lost the eye. Each one thought the other had it. They began to bicker about it.

Just then Perseus spoke up. He demanded to know where the fairies of the North were. Perseus promised to return the eye as soon as they told him.

They gave him directions at once. The Gray Women would have done anything to get their eye back. As soon as he had his directions, Perseus returned it to them.

"Good job," Hermes said to Perseus. "Now let's find the fairies of the North." They continued their journey. Hermes kept talking. "Once the fairies tell you where the Gorgons live, I will give you a sword to attack Medusa. The sword cannot be bent or broken by the Gorgons' golden scales."

Hermes's sword was a wonderful gift. *But what good will this sword be when the Gorgons can turn me to stone instantly?* Perseus thought.

Athena, the goddess of war, heard his thoughts. She realized the problem and came to help. She appeared in front of Hermes and Perseus. Athena took off her polished bronze shield and held it out.

"Look into this when you attack Medusa," she said. "It will act as a mirror and you will be able to see her reflection. This way you will not have to look at her directly. You will avoid her deadly power and not be turned into stone."

Now Perseus had hope that he would be able to fight the Gorgons. He felt confident during the long journey.

Perseus and Hermes came to the land of the fairies of the North. Perseus was amazed at how good, generous, and happy they were. The fairies showed him great kindness. They welcomed him with a feast. They told him exactly how to reach the Gorgons' lair. And they gave him three gifts. One was a pair of winged sandals. Another was a magic silver purse that changed size to fit whatever Perseus needed to carry. And most important, they gave him a cap that would make him invisible. With these gifts—plus Athena's shield and Hermes's sword—Perseus was ready to meet the Gorgons.

Hermes flew with Perseus to the home of the Gorgons.

The Gorgons were asleep when Perseus found them. He could see them clearly in the mirror of Athena's shield. They were just as Polydectes had described. The Gorgons had great wings. Their bodies were covered with golden scales. And their hair was a mass of twisting snakes. They were more terrible than he could have imagined.

Athena and Hermes stood on either side of Perseus. They pointed out Medusa. She was the only one of the three Gorgons who could be killed. The other two were immortal.

Perseus hovered above the Gorgons on

his winged sandals. He looked at them only through the mirrored shield. Perseus aimed Hermes's sword at Medusa's throat. Athena guided his hand. He cut through Medusa's neck with the sword. Then he swooped low enough to grab her head. Perseus looked into the shield the whole time. By doing that, he avoided being turned into stone.

Perseus dropped Medusa's head into his magical purse. It closed around the head. There was nothing to fear from Medusa now. At that moment the other two Gorgons awoke. Horrified at the sight of Perseus, they tried to fight him. But Perseus slipped his magical cap onto his head. He became invisible, and the monsters could not find him.

Happy and proud, Perseus returned to his tiny fishing village. He expected to find his mother married and living happily with Polydectes. Instead, his mother was missing. Polydectes had become terrible and cruel to those who lived on the island. Perseus was furious.

"I know what I must do," Perseus said to himself. He went to Polydectes's palace. Perseus entered the front hall and slammed the door. He stood at the entrance, holding Athena's shield on his chest. The silver purse with Medusa's head was at his side. Every man in the hall, including Polydectes, looked at him.

Before anyone could look away, Perseus held up Medusa's head in front of him. In that moment the cruel king and all his servants turned to stone. Perseus quickly placed Medusa's head back in the silver purse.

The people who lived on the island celebrated. They were free from the cruel king.

But Perseus was not celebrating. He still could not find his mother.

"She went into hiding after you left," explained one of the villagers.

"She refused to marry Polydectes. She said she did not love him. And so he threatened to kill her," said another.

News traveled fast throughout the island. Danae learned that Perseus had turned Polydectes into stone. She finally came out of hiding. Mother and son were happily reunited. They were never separated again for the rest of their lives.

CHAPTER 10

Theseus and the Minotaur

A long time ago in Athens, a child was to be born to the king, Aegeus. The king wanted to protect his unborn child from his brutal enemies. So he brought his pregnant wife to her home in southern Greece. There she could raise their child in safety, far away from his enemies in Athens.

King Aegeus was afraid he might never have the chance to know his child. So he placed a special sword in a cave. Next to it, he placed a special pair of shoes. He covered the entrance to the cave with a heavy stone. Before King Aegeus left his pregnant wife to go back to Athens, he told her what he had done.

"If we have a son, tell him to come to this cave when he grows strong enough. See if he can roll away the stone and get the things behind it. If so, send him to Athens. He may then claim me as his father."

Soon the child was born. It was a boy, and his mother named him Theseus. The boy grew up stronger than all others. When his mother finally took him to the cave, he had no trouble moving the stone. He saw the great sword and shoes inside.

"The time has come for you to find your father," his mother told him. "Your grandfather will give you a ship. Sail to Athens swiftly and safely. Do not take the road. The road to Athens is long and full of dangerous robbers."

"No, Mother, I will not take the easy way to

Athens. I want to be like my cousin Heracles. Heracles would not travel by sea," Theseus told her.

Theseus walked for many days on the road to Athens. He came across many thieves who robbed innocent, poor people. Theseus fought each of them and won. Soon all of Greece rang with praise for the young man. News traveled that Theseus had brought justice to all the villains in the land.

By the time Theseus reached Athens, everyone thought he was a hero. King Aegeus was not aware that Theseus was his son. He had never met him, nor did he know his son's name. The king was jealous that the young man was so popular. He was afraid the people of Athens might like Theseus better than him.

So King Aegeus talked to his adviser, Medea the sorceress. Medea had once helped Jason obtain the Golden Fleece with her magical powers. She eventually began using her magical powers to help King Aegeus run his kingdom.

Medea knew that Theseus was King Aegeus's son. Her magical powers helped her know many things. But she was afraid that if the king learned Theseus was his son, he would have no need for her anymore. The king asked Medea what he should do about this young hero.

"Invite him to a special banquet, my king. I will serve him a poisoned drink," Medea said in her soothing voice. "With the young hero gone, there will be no threat to your kingship. And I promise you, no one will ever know."

The king invited Theseus to the palace for a banquet that night. When the young man arrived, Medea offered the poisoned drink to him. But at that moment Theseus drew his sword to show King Aegeus. He wanted the king to know who he was.

Of course, the king instantly recognized the

sword as his own. He knocked the poisoned drink out of Medea's hand. It fell to the ground.

"How dare you try to poison my son!" the king roared at Medea.

Medea realized that her evil plan had been discovered. She fled the room and escaped from Athens.

King Aegeus then declared that Theseus was his son and next in line for the throne. Just then a messenger from King Minos arrived. He came from the island of Crete, where King Minos ruled. The messenger demanded the usual offering of seven young women and seven young men.

"Father, what does the messenger mean by this?" Theseus asked.

"It is a terrible curse upon our kingdom, my son." King Aegeus told him the story.

Years ago, King Minos's son had visited King Aegeus. But Aegeus didn't welcome the prince to his land. Instead, he had sent the young man on a dangerous mission to kill a wild bull. The bull killed the prince. Then King Minos attacked Athens and King Aegeus.

Aegeus begged Minos for his life and his kingdom. Minos insisted Aegeus make up for the death of his son. He demanded that Athens send seven young women and seven young men to Crete every nine years. These young Athenians would enter a labyrinth, or giant maze, made out of tall bushes. There the Athenians would be eaten by the Minotaur—a half-human, half-bull monster—for the entertainment of Minos's people. Although it pained him, King Aegeus agreed to King Minos's demand.

"Why can't the young women and men escape from the labyrinth?" Theseus asked his father.

"It was made by Daedalus. He is a great inventor and architect. Daedalus is the most skillful man in the world," King Aegeus explained. "To escape from the labyrinth made of bushes is impossible. Its pathways twist and turn in endless ways. No one can ever find their way out without crossing the Minotaur's path," he added sadly.

"Let me go as part of the offering," Theseus said. "I will kill the Minotaur and end this deadly agreement."

"My son, you have just arrived! You are prince of the kingdom. I cannot lose you so quickly," King Aegeus cried.

"Father, I promise you I will return," Theseus told him. "I must go. I will not take no for an answer." King Aegeus had to let Theseus go.

Theseus and the thirteen other men and women traveled to Crete. When they arrived, King Minos's daughter Ariadne fell in love with Theseus instantly. In the same moment, she became troubled. She knew Theseus had come to enter the labyrinth. He would have to meet the Minotaur. Ariadne sent for Daedalus at once.

"You must tell me how to escape from the labyrinth," she insisted.

At first, Daedalus would not. He was afraid that King Minos would find out and punish him.

"I promise, your secret will be safe with me," Ariadne told him. At last Daedalus gave her the secret.

The next day, the fourteen young women and men from Athens would enter the labyrinth. There was a grand ceremony planned for the event. Before dawn, Ariadne went down to the prison where Theseus and the others were being kept.

"Theseus, I have found a way for you to escape the Minotaur and the labyrinth. I will tell you if you promise me one thing," Ariadne said.

"Yes, Princess. What do you want from me?" Theseus asked.

"Take me back to Athens with you. Marry me and love me forever. If you promise this, I will tell you what you need to know," she whispered.

"I promise," Theseus whispered back.

Ariadne handed Theseus a ball of thread.

"Are you playing a joke on me, Princess? What can I do with this?" Theseus asked.

"Fasten one end of the thread to the entrance of the labyrinth. Unwind it as you go. It will help you find your way back out," she told him.

Theseus gratefully took the ball of thread. That day, he did exactly as Ariadne had told him. Theseus tied the string as he entered the labyrinth. Then he boldly walked in. He unwound the thread as he went. Theseus finally came upon the hideous Minotaur. It was fast asleep in the center of the labyrinth. Before the

Minotaur could wake, Theseus threw himself upon the monster, hitting it with his bare fists.

The Minotaur fought back. It snorted and snarled. It thrashed its hooves. It gnashed its teeth. There was a terrible struggle. But Theseus was strong, and the Minotaur was not prepared for this battle.

After fighting long and hard, Theseus won. The Minotaur was finally dead.

Theseus retraced his steps through the labyrinth. Thanks to Ariadne, he could follow the thread he had unwound along the way. He led all the other young women and men out of the labyrinth. They stepped into the sunlight. Ariadne joined them.

Before King Minos could find out what had happened, Theseus quickly led all of them to their ship. The ship was still waiting in the harbor. The group set sail for Athens at once. Luck was with them. A strong wind blew them fast from the shores of Crete. Soon they were out in the open sea.

They were safe at last! Athens would never again have to send any more young people to the labyrinth. No one would have to face the Minotaur again.

Theseus kept his promise to Ariadne. As soon as they arrived in Athens, they married. And Theseus eventually became king of Athens. He was a wise and gentle king and was loved by his people.

CHAPTER 11

Daedalus and Icarus

Daedalus was the great architect and inventor who worked for King Minos. He had made a labyrinth of bushes that housed the terrible Minotaur.

King Minos learned that the Athenians had escaped from the labyrinth and killed his Minotaur. He was in a rage. He also knew whom to blame. Only Daedalus could have helped them escape. Only he knew the secret to escaping the maze.

As punishment, King Minos trapped Daedalus

and his son Icarus in the labyrinth. They had only the clothes on their backs and a pair of candles to light their way.

Daedalus tried to lead his son through the endless paths of the maze. But he could not. Not without the ball of string he had given to Ariadne.

"Father, it is no use," Icarus said with a sigh. "You have invented a maze that is too winding. Not even you can find your way out."

Daedalus was about to give up when he looked up to the gods for an answer. And then it came to him! The labyrinth had many walls, but no ceiling.

"I have an idea, my son!" Daedalus told him with excitement. "If we can't escape by land, we can escape by flying!"

"We are not birds, Father. We cannot fly," Icarus pointed out.

But Daedalus didn't listen. He was too

busy gathering branches and leaves from the labyrinth's bushes. Daedalus began stringing them together.

"Icarus, see these bird feathers that have fluttered down from the sky? Gather up as many as you can," Daedalus told his son.

In a few minutes, Daedalus had made two pairs of wings. There was one set for each of them. He fastened a pair onto Icarus's arms. Then he put on the other pair of wings.

"Listen carefully, Icarus," Daedalus said. "These wings are fragile. They are held together only with candle wax. You must not fly too high in the sky. Stay away from the sun. If you get too close, the wax will melt. Your wings will come undone and drop off," he warned.

But Icarus wasn't listening. He was too excited and busy flapping his new wings. Daedalus took off into the sky. At first, Icarus followed closely behind his father.

For a while, father and son flew side by side. They easily escaped the labyrinth and Crete. They flew over land and sea. Soon they were far away from King Minos's kingdom.

"Father, look at me!" Icarus cried. He did a somersault through the air. He swooped down one minute. Then he soared high up the next. Flying was such a thrill to Icarus.

"See how high I can fly!" Icarus called. He flew closer to the sun.

"Icarus! The sun! Stay away from the sun!" Daedalus cried. Feathers from Icarus's wings began drifting down past Daedalus.

"Come back!" Daedalus shouted. But Icarus did not hear him.

Icarus did not see the feathers fall from his wings. He did not see the wax melt and drip. He was too excited to be flying. Icarus's wings came apart. He could fly no longer. He fell down, down, down into the sea.

"Icarus!" Daedalus cried out. He flew down to try to catch him. But Icarus plunged into the sea. The water closed up around him. Daedalus could no longer see his son.

Daedalus flew to the spot he had last seen Icarus. He called out his name till his voice was hoarse. He stayed there for hours, hoping Icarus would come to the surface.

Finally, he knew Icarus would never come up again. Daedalus flew away and eventually landed in Sicily. He lived there for the rest of his life. But he was so heartbroken over Icarus that he never invented another thing again.

CHAPTER 12

Phaeton and Apollo

⌒

The palace of Apollo, the sun god, was radiant. It shone with gold, gleamed with ivory, and sparkled with jewels. Everything in it flashed, glowed, and glittered. It was always high noon. Darkness and night were unknown there.

Very few gods and mortals could bear the brightness. Most mortals had never been there.

One day, a young boy named Phaeton dared to approach Apollo's palace. The boy had a very important question to ask the sun god. On his way, Phaeton had to stop many times to cover his eyes. But he had decided that he must come face-to-face with Apollo.

Phaeton finally arrived at Apollo's palace. He burst through the heavy doors into the throne room. There sat Apollo the sun god. The god was surrounded by a blazing light. Phaeton was forced to stop. The light was blinding.

"Why are you here, my boy?" Apollo asked kindly.

"I have come to ask you a very important question." Phaeton took a small step forward. "Are you my true father?" he asked. "My mother said that you were. But the other boys at school laugh at me when I say that I am your son. They will not believe me. When I told that to my mother, she told me to go ask you!"

Smiling, Apollo took off his crown of burning light. He wanted Phaeton to be able to look at him directly.

"Come here, Phaeton," Apollo called. "You

are my son. Your mother told you the truth. I will give you proof. Ask anything you want from me and you shall have it, I promise. And gods must always keep their promises," Apollo told him.

Phaeton had often watched the sun god throughout the day. Apollo rode through the sky on his fiery chariot. This excited and amazed Phaeton. He always wondered what it would be like to drive that chariot. What was it like to guide the noble horses? What would it be like to bring light to the world?

"Father!" he cried. "I choose to drive your chariot. Just for one day. Let me have your chariot," Phaeton begged.

At once, Apollo realized he had made a big mistake.

"My dear boy—" Apollo began, shaking his head.

"It is the only thing I want, Father," Phaeton interrupted.

"And this is the only thing I would refuse you," Apollo answered.

"You promised," Phaeton reminded him.

"Listen to me, Phaeton," Apollo said. "It is too dangerous. You are half mortal. No mortal can drive my chariot. No god can drive it, either, except for me. Even Zeus, the ruler of the gods, cannot drive my chariot."

"But, Father—" Phaeton started to say.

"Consider the road, my son. It rises up from the sea so steeply. Even the horses can hardly climb it. In the middle of the sky, the road is so high. Even I do not like to look toward the ground. Worst of all is the way back down. It is so dangerous that Poseidon wonders how I do not fall out of my chariot and into the waters," Apollo explained.

"I don't care," Phaeton pouted. "I want to drive the chariot. It's all I want."

"Guiding the horses is almost impossible," Apollo added. "Their fiery spirits grow hotter as they climb. I can barely control them myself. Be reasonable, Phaeton. How could you drive the chariot when I can hardly do it? Please do not ask me to grant this wish.

"Do you think there are wonders and beautiful things at the end of the sun's road? Is that why you want to drive the chariot?" Apollo wanted to know. "There aren't. You have to pass fierce, dangerous beasts. The Bull, the Lion, the Scorpion, the great Crab—each one of them will try to harm you.

"My son, I would give you anything else in the world. Choose anything else and I will make it yours," Apollo said.

Apollo's words were not heard. Phaeton saw himself proudly standing in that chariot. He saw himself guiding those fiery horses that even Zeus could not control. He didn't care about the dangers his father had described. He was not afraid.

"You promised," Phaeton said.

Apollo grew silent. It was hopeless. Phaeton would not change his mind.

"If you will not change your mind, we must hurry," Apollo said. "It is almost time."

The gates of the East glowed purple. Dawn had appeared, full of rosy light. The stars were just leaving the sky. The morning star was growing dim.

The Seasons stood at the gates, waiting to open them. Apollo's horses had already been tied to the chariot. They were waiting for their driver. And they were not patient.

With pride and joy, Phaeton climbed into the chariot. He took hold of the reins. In an flash, he was off!

The horses' hooves tore through the low-hanging mist above the sea. Then the horses brought the chariot up through the clean, crisp air. Up and up Phaeton rode. The chariot was climbing to the height of Heaven. For a few moments, Phaeton felt like the lord of the sky. Then suddenly there was a change.

The chariot swung wildly to and fro. The horses raced faster and faster. Phaeton lost control of the reins. The horses ran wilder and faster than before. They knew now that they were in control, not Phaeton.

The horses left the path and rushed wherever they wanted. Up, down, right, left—they nearly crashed the chariot into the Scorpion. They stopped short just before they ran into the great Crab. Phaeton was dizzy with terror. He let the reins drop.

The horses ran even more madly and more out of control. They soared to the very top of

the sky. Then they plunged down to the earth. They set the world on fire.

The highest mountains were the first to burn. The flame ran down these slopes to the lands below. Low valleys and dark forests caught fire. Soon everything was in flames. The streams turned into steam. The rivers dried up.

Phaeton could hardly stay inside the chariot now. He was covered in thick ash. The heat and smoke were too much for him. Phaeton wished the torment and terror would end.

It looked as if there was no hope left for Phaeton. But Mother Earth noticed that he was in trouble. She cried out to the gods for help. Her cry reached all the way to the top of Mount Olympus. The gods looked down and realized they must act quickly. Otherwise the chariot would bring the whole world crashing down.

Zeus threw his lightning bolt at Phaeton. It struck him, shattered the chariot, and made the crazed horses run into the sea. Phaeton fell from the chariot to the earth. The mysterious, unknown River Eridanus received him and cooled his body.

Nearby wood creatures took pity on Phaeton. They placed him in a bed of moss and carved a stone tribute to him. On it were the words:

Here lies Phaeton, who drove the sun god's chariot. Greatly he failed, but greatly he had dared.

CHAPTER 13

King Midas

ᴄᴏ

Once there lived a king named Midas. He lived in the kingdom of Phrygia, which was also known as the land of roses. He was very proud of his great rose garden. He did not allow anyone, except his family, to enter the garden.

One night, an old man named Silenus lost his way. Silenus was a friend of the god Dionysus. He wandered into the palace grounds and found Midas's rose garden. The next morning, the palace servants found him asleep in a bed of roses. His arms and legs were sprawled out, and he looked very silly.

"Who can this be?" asked one servant.

"Looks a bit like Dionysus," said another.

"I have an idea," said the first servant. "Let's present this silly old man to the king."

"That will give us a good laugh," said the other.

So the servants dressed Silenus in roses and vines. They put a flowery wreath on his head. Then they woke him up and took him to King Midas.

King Midas was a generous person. So he welcomed the strange man into his palace. For ten days, the king entertained the silly old man Silenus. He fed him delicious food and made sure the old man was comfortable. And Silenus also entertained Midas, telling stories and singing songs. The servants watched with amusement.

King Midas gave Silenus anything he would ask for.

"Bring me another plate of food, Midas," Silenus called.

"Yes, of course," Midas replied.

"Five pillows and a fur blanket, Midas," Silenus shouted.

"Right away," Midas answered. He had his servants deliver to Silenus anything he wanted.

At the end of the ten days, Midas offered to take Silenus back to Dionysus. Silenus agreed that it was time to go. Midas put Silenus on a horse and led him to Dionysus's temple.

Dionysus was delighted to have his old friend back. He offered to reward King Midas for taking such good care of Silenus.

"As a gift for returning Silenus to me, I will make your wish come true," Dionysus said. "Tell me, what is your one wish?"

Without a second thought, Midas said, "I want everything I touch to turn to gold."

Dionysus knew this was a bad idea. He knew exactly what would happen to Midas if he granted this wish. But he was not supposed to correct anyone's wishes.

"So it shall be from this day forward that everything you touch turns to gold," Dionysus said, granting the wish.

Midas hurried back to his palace and rose garden. He was very pleased with himself. Midas wanted to tell his family the good news. Their kingdom would now be richer than any other kingdom.

When he returned, Midas asked the palace chef to cook the biggest, best breakfast he ever cooked. The kitchen servants hurried about. They brought heaping plates of meats and eggs. They carried out large platters of fruits. And they sent to the table bottles filled with delicious drinks.

Midas picked up a juicy piece of chicken and put it to his mouth. He bit down and—*crack!* Lo and behold, there was no meat on the bone at all. In its place was a thick and solid piece of gold.

Midas reached for one of the bottles. He was very thirsty. The moment Midas touched it, the whole thing became a lump of solid gold.

"What have I done?" Midas cried out.

He was so hungry and thirsty. There was food all around him. Yet he could not eat a thing.

"This golden touch is a curse," Midas cried aloud.

Just then Midas's daughter entered the palace dining room. He loved her more than anything in the world. She was as good as the king was greedy.

"Father, what is it?" she asked, coming to his side.

Before he could stop himself, Midas reached out to hug his daughter. And in that instant, she turned into a golden statue.

Midas was beside himself with sadness. He wept and wept. He held his daughter to him, but she could not hug him back. His only daughter was trapped in gold. The worst part was that Midas knew he was the one to blame. He could hardly bear it!

Dionysus saw this happening and felt bad. He took pity on the old king. Dionysus came to Midas's palace. He whispered in the king's ear the secret to curing his golden touch.

"Wash yourself and your daughter in the oldest river, Pactolus. It will cure you of your golden touch. Your daughter will become human again," Dionysus told him.

Midas did just as Dionysus said. He brought the golden statue of his daughter down to the river. Carefully he lowered her into the water.

Within moments, his daughter was back to normal. Midas rejoiced and hugged his daughter tightly. He vowed to himself that for the rest of his days he would never be so greedy again.

CHAPTER 14

Atalanta

Long ago, a little girl was born in the land of Arcady, in Greece. Her name was Atalanta. When she was a baby, her father brought her with him on a hunting trip. He left her alone on a wild mountainside while he went off to hunt. Night came and the baby girl grew cold and hungry. Her father did not return. She began to cry.

A she-bear broke through the wild bushes and trees. The animal headed straight for the crying baby. The she-bear scooped up the little girl. Gently, she cradled the baby in her paws and brought her back to the bear cave. The she-bear nursed the baby girl, kept her warm, and raised her as if she was her very own bear cub.

Soon Atalanta was old enough to move freely on her own over the mountainside. The she-bear had raised her to be a daring and mischievous little girl.

Atalanta loved to run fast and play hide-and-seek with the bears. No matter where Atalanta hid, the she-bear could always find her.

Early one morning, before the bears awoke, Atalanta left the bear cave. She went to search for a new hiding place. Atalanta went far away to find the perfect spot. At last she came to a deep hole in the ground. It was covered with branches and leaves.

This is the perfect hiding place, she thought to herself. *She-bear and the cubs will never find me here.* Atalanta giggled.

Then she jumped right in. The deep, dark

hole smelled of wet leaves and earth. Atalanta waited and waited. The she-bear and the cubs did not come. The sun moved across the sky. It was now the middle of the day. Atalanta began to get hungry. And still the she-bear and the cubs did not come.

Suddenly Atalanta heard footsteps. She stayed very still. Then she heard a shifting of earth and the scraping of branches. A bit of sunlight fell into the dark hole.

Atalanta looked up. Instead of the she-bear, Atalanta saw an unfamiliar sight.

"It's not a bear cub we've been tracking at all," said a deep voice.

"Why, it's a little girl," exclaimed another.

Two pairs of strong arms pulled Atalanta from the deep hole. She was curious about the strange creatures.

"Here you go," said one of them. He held up a loaf of bread in one hand and a sweet honey treat in the other. Atalanta was so hungry that she ate the food quickly. The two kind men smiled at her.

"A little girl like you shouldn't be in the woods by herself," one of the men said.

"We'll take you home. Our families will care for you properly," said the other.

The two kind men and their wives took Atalanta in. They taught her to hunt and fish. Soon she became more skilled than them.

By the time Atalanta was a young woman, she could run, hunt, and wrestle better than any young man in all of Greece.

One day Atalanta was walking in the woods. Two Centaurs caught sight of her. Centaurs were creatures that were half human, half horse. They had nasty tempers and often attacked humans. Atalanta saw the two creatures running toward her at full speed. It was a terrifying sight. But

Atalanta was not afraid. Did she turn and run? She did not.

Atalanta stood perfectly still. Calmly, she fitted an arrow to her bow. She pulled back the bowstring and sent the first arrow whistling through the air. Down went the first Centaur. Without a pause, Atalanta restrung her bow. She sent a second arrow through the air. Down went the second Centaur. The terrible creatures were dead. The people of the land were finally safe.

One day, Atalanta learned that the king of Caledonia had sent out a call for help. All the young men in Greece got his message. His land was troubled by a great boar. Years ago, he had forgotten to make a sacrifice to Artemis in thanks for their harvest. Artemis was angry with the kingdom. She sent the boar to punish the king.

Atalanta traveled to Caledonia. She wanted to see if she could help the king and his people. When Atalanta arrived, she saw many young men gathered at the palace. The men had come from every part of Greece. Much to their surprise, Atalanta walked right into the center of the group.

"I am here to hunt the great Caledonian Boar," she announced. Everyone looked at her with great curiosity.

Atalanta wore a simple robe clasped with a shiny buckle. An ivory tube hung over her left shoulder. That was where she carried her arrows. She held her bow in her other hand. Her lovely hair was pushed back from her face and tied with a single ribbon.

"Who does she think she is?" asked one young man.

"Go away, girl! Get back to your home," said another.

"Do you think you are Artemis herself?" joked another. The men laughed at the young girl who thought she was a hunter.

"Who is that pretty maiden?" whispered Meleager, son of the king.

"I am Atalanta of Arcady," she announced. "I am here to hunt the great Caledonian Boar."

"Ridiculous," said another young man. "We should not have to hunt with a woman!"

"Silence!" Prince Meleager said. "If the maiden wants to come with us, she shall."

The group of young men grumbled under their breath. But they obeyed the prince.

"Thank you," Atalanta said to Prince Meleager with a smile.

"Atalanta, please join us at the castle for dinner before tomorrow's hunt," the kind prince offered.

Atalanta happily agreed. All through dinner, Prince Meleager gazed at her. He was falling in love with her.

"Father, she is so lovely. I would like to

marry her. May I have your permission?" Prince Meleager asked the king.

"I have heard of Atalanta, the pride of Arcady. She is a skilled huntress. She has strength and spirit. She runs like the wind and roams the countryside as she pleases. She is not like other young women. Many have asked to marry her. Marriage is not what she wants," the king warned.

"Even so, I must ask her," Prince Meleager answered. "I will, after the hunt."

Before dawn the next morning, the group got together to begin the hunt for the boar. They crept through the forest and listened carefully for snuffling sounds. This would signal that the great wild boar was close.

A great mist settled over the forest. The hunters could barely see a few feet in front of them. Many grew nervous and became confused.

They stumbled over one another. No longer were they in a proper hunting position.

Just then, out of the mist, came a loud crash. The great Caledonian Boar burst through the trees. It raced straight toward the crowd of hunters.

The boar speared two hunters with its tusks. It shook them like rag dolls until they were limp. The boar then tossed them into the forest and turned to the other hunters.

The young men shouted and ran in every direction. They stumbled upon one another. Their arrows rained through the air. None of them hit the boar.

Only Atalanta remained calm. She fitted her arrow to her bow. Then she let it fly, straight and true, into the great boar's side.

The beast shrieked and stumbled for just a moment. Prince Meleager took that chance to throw his spear and put an end to the horrible beast.

At last, Caledonia was free from the terrible curse of the great boar! Everyone was so happy. The beast had destroyed their land for a long time. Now they would have a plentiful harvest.

At the celebration dinner that night, Prince Meleager spoke with Atalanta.

"Lovely Atalanta, you are so brave and beautiful. You have helped me rid my land of the cursed boar. Marry me so we can rule the land together," Prince Meleager said.

Atalanta blushed a deep red.

"My prince, I am honored that you would choose me. But I will never marry. I am a huntress and I roam the land as I please. I am not right for marriage to any man," Atalanta replied.

Prince Meleager could not believe his ears.

"I will tell you what I have told others before you. I will only marry the man who can beat me in a race," Atalanta said.

"I have offered you my kingdom," Prince Meleager said. "Is that not enough?"

Atalanta did not want to hurt his feelings any more. She shook her head and bowed before him.

"I must go," she said in a quiet voice.

"Then we shall have a race!" Prince Meleager declared. "And I shall win it and your love."

The next morning, Atalanta appeared, ready to race against the prince. A crowd gathered to watch. She waited and waited. Prince Meleager did not come.

"Where is the prince?" murmured someone in the crowd.

"Perhaps he is sick," said someone else.

"Perhaps he has forgotten," said another person.

The truth was somewhere in between.

Prince Meleager's mother was a powerful sorceress. When she had married the king, the queen kept her magic powers a secret. She used them rarely.

The queen heard about Meleager and Atalanta's race. She became angry.

"What is this I hear? Our son has offered to run a race? To win some peasant girl's hand in marriage?" she asked the king.

"The boy loves her dearly," the king said, defending his son.

"I have heard that she was brought up by a she-bear," the queen remarked. "I've heard that she has roamed wild in the countryside since she was a child. This girl is not a suitable princess for our son," she added.

Prince Meleager overheard his mother and father talking.

"Mother, she is not just any girl. She is the

bravest, strongest, and most beautiful girl in all of Greece," Meleager told her.

"She has enchanted you," the queen said.

"She's done nothing like that," Meleager said.

"What if you do not win this silly race? Have you thought of that?" the queen asked. "Would you embarrass yourself, your father, and your kingdom over this girl?"

"I am old enough to decide whom I will marry. I truly love Atalanta. I tell you, I will embarrass no one. I shall beat her in the race tomorrow and make her my bride!" Prince Meleager said. He stormed out of the room to prepare for the race.

"Let the boy do as he wishes. There is no harm in it. The girl is lovely. Although she may be swift, she is still just a girl. Meleager is strong and even faster than she. He will win the race and the girl. And then he will be very happy," said the king.

"As you wish, my king," the queen said to her husband.

But that night, after everyone was asleep, the queen crept into Prince Meleager's bedroom. She stood over his bed and placed a magic spell on him as he slept.

"Son of mine you will always be. From Atalanta I will set you free!" The queen spoke this spell three times. "Sleep well, my son. Think of marriage no more."

The next day, Prince Meleager slept too late. He missed the race. When he did wake, he had forgotten all about the race. He forgot about wanting to marry Atalanta.

The queen told the king that Meleager had changed his mind. From that day on, no one ever spoke another word about the race, marriage, or Atalanta.

When Atalanta realized that the prince would not race, she started to leave.

"Wait," said a young man. "I am Hippomenes. I have admired you from the moment I saw you. I love you for your beauty and strength. May I race you for your hand in marriage?" he asked.

Atalanta looked into the deep, dark eyes of this strong and handsome young man. She had not noticed him before. Her cheeks blushed.

"You will lose," Atalanta warned him. "Just as so many others have before you."

"Unlike the prince of Caledonia, I am willing to take that risk," Hippomenes said with a smile.

"Then we shall race," Atalanta said, smiling in return.

Atalanta did not know that Hippomenes had come prepared to race her. He had brought three golden apples from a secret garden. No one—mortal or god—could resist these golden apples.

Atalanta and Hippomenes stood on the race course. They waited for the starting signal.

Crack! came the sound of a walking stick smacked against a tree. The two runners set off.

Atalanta ran as swiftly as one of her arrows shot through the air. Her hair blew over her shoulders in the wind.

Hippomenes was one step behind her.

As Atalanta was about to pull ahead, Hippomenes rolled a golden apple in front of her.

It glittered in the sunlight. Atalanta saw it and had to have it. She stopped and picked up the apple. It only took a moment. That was enough for Hippomenes to catch up to her.

Atalanta ran faster. Again, she began to pull ahead. Again, Hippomenes rolled a golden apple in her path. Atalanta had to swerve off the path to get the golden apple. As she scooped it up, Hippomenes raced past her.

Back on the race path, Atalanta ran quicker than she had ever run before. She caught up to Hippomenes. The finish line was in her sight.

Hippomenes knew this was his last chance. Once again, he rolled a golden apple in her path. This time, the apple rolled into the grass on the side of the road.

Atalanta could not resist the golden apple that flashed before her. She reached for the fruit. Hippomenes burst forward. He crossed the finish line and won the race! Atalanta was his. Her days as a free hunter and wanderer were over.

Atalanta and Hippomenes lived happily for a little while. They had a son. He eventually grew up to be a great hero.

One day, Zeus and Aphrodite overheard Atalanta and Hippomenes boasting to others about their son.

"He is as mighty as Zeus," Hippomenes said.

"And handsome enough to marry Aphrodite, or any goddess," Atalanta added.

Zeus and Aphrodite looked at each other in

surprise. The pride of Hippomenes and Atalanta shocked them.

"How dare they?" Zeus shouted.

"We should punish them for their proud words," Aphrodite suggested.

"What shall we do?" Zeus wondered.

Zeus and Aphrodite thought about it for a while. They decided on the perfect punishment for Hippomenes and Atalanta.

Zeus sent a mighty rainstorm their way. It forced Hippomenes and Atalanta to run for cover. Then Zeus threw down several lightning bolts. He hit both of them, and—*poof!* He turned Hippomenes, Atalanta, and their son into surprised lions.

The family forever after roamed the countryside as lions. They spent the rest of their days as a "pride," which is what a lion's family is called. They were never seen in human form again.

CHAPTER 15

Pegasus and Bellerophon

In the great Greek city of Corinth lived a young man named Bellerophon. His mother was a mortal. But she was equal in wit and wisdom to any goddess. And Bellerophon was so bold, clever, and handsome. Everyone believed he was the son of Poseidon.

As Bellerophon grew up, he heard much talk of a horrible beast, the Chimera.

The Chimera was a winged creature of great strength and speed. She was a lion in front, a goat in the middle, and a serpent in the back. Her

breath was an unstoppable flame. It would burn anyone who came before her. She traveled from city to city. All humans were terrified of her. Every city lived in fear of the Chimera's arrival.

The people of Corinth learned that the Chimera was on her way. There was much panic throughout the city.

"What shall we do?" murmured one of the city residents.

"We need a hero," another said.

"Bellerophon!" someone shouted.

The rest of the crowd started chanting his

name. "Bellerophon! Bellerophon! Bellerophon!"

Bellerophon appeared to the crowd after hearing his name called.

"My people, what do you want from me?" he asked.

"The Chimera is on its way. You must save us. You must kill it!" the crowd shouted.

Bellerophon knew of the terrible Chimera. The monster would float in the sky. She would breathe fire upon the city until it burned to the ground. Bellerophon knew it was almost impossible to get near this monster. But he also knew he could not let his people suffer.

"I will do my best," Bellerophon said.

Still, he wondered how he was going to defeat this monster. No other mortal had been able to kill the Chimera.

Bellerophon thought of the great and mighty winged horse, Pegasus. The magical horse lived near the famous spring in Corinth. If only he could tame and ride Pegasus, he might have a chance against the Chimera. But how would he do it? No one had ever been able to capture Pegasus.

So Bellerophon went to see a prophet, the Wise One. Every Greek hero has turned to the Wise One for answers to tough questions.

"To capture the great winged horse and defeat the Chimera, you need two things," the Wise One said. "A pair of soft slippers and a golden harness."

"How will these things help?" Bellerophon asked. But the Wise One would say no more.

Bellerophon asked his mother for a soft pair of slippers. She gladly gave them to him.

Next, he went to the temple of Athena and asked her for a golden harness. He waited, but none appeared. He waited so long that he fell asleep in front of the goddess's temple. He dreamed of a golden harness.

Athena saw the beautiful boy asleep at her temple. She looked into his dream and saw the golden harness in his thoughts. Athena took pity on Bellerophon. She decided she would help him.

While he slept, Athena made a golden harness that would fit Pegasus perfectly. When Bellerophon awoke, a golden harness lay beside the boy.

Bellerophon was sure now that the gods were with him. He set out to capture Pegasus so he could defeat the terrible Chimera.

When Bellerophon arrived at the spring, he saw the wonderful winged horse. She was drinking quietly. Bellerophon walked right over to Pegasus. His footsteps were too loud, though. Pegasus became frightened and flew straight up in the air and far away.

Bellerophon hid behind a bush until Pegasus grew thirsty again. Once again, the winged horse settled down to drink at the spring.

This time, Bellerophon took off his shoes. He put on the soft slippers his mother had given him. Bellerophon crept softly until he was just behind the winged horse. Quickly he slipped the golden harness over Pegasus's head. The flying horse did not try to fly away this time. Instead, Pegasus calmly turned to Bellerophon and gazed at him.

"There you go," Bellerophon whispered, petting Pegasus. "You are a beauty," he added.

Pegasus seemed to understand his words. She bowed her head and knelt before him. Bellerophon leaped onto the winged horse's back. Off they flew.

Meanwhile, the Chimera had settled in the sky over Corinth. Her lion's head roared a terrible roar. It rumbled throughout the city, shaking houses and scorching gardens.

"Where is Bellerophon?" the people of Corinth cried.

The Chimera breathed fire. It poured down like rain upon the city.

"We are doomed," the people shouted.

Just then Bellerophon appeared in the sky upon the back of Pegasus.

"We will save the people of Corinth," Bellerophon shouted.

Bellerophon told Pegasus to fly circles around the Chimera. This would distract the monster from harming the city further.

Pegasus and Bellerophon circled the Chimera. The great beast spun around and around in the air. She roared. She hissed. She kicked. But Bellerophon and Pegasus were too swift for the horrible creature. She could not catch them. The Chimera grew dizzy. She hung in midair.

At that moment, Bellerophon put his arrow to his bow and let it fly. The arrow flew straight into the horrible monster's heart. The Chimera dropped to the ground.

She did not roar like a lion. She did not hiss fire like a serpent. She did not kick like a goat. She lay perfectly still.

The citizens of Corinth shouted, "Bellerophon has saved us! Bellerophon is our hero!"

The people cheered, clapped, and hugged one another. They were saved. Bellerophon bowed his head in thanks. But he knew the truth.

"You are the real hero," Bellerophon whispered to Pegasus. "Without you, I could not have defeated the Chimera."

Pegasus neighed softly. It almost sounded like "thank you" to Bellerophon.

From that day on, Pegasus and Bellerophon fought many monsters. They had many more adventures. But their most famous battle was with the Chimera. The people of Corinth have never forgotten their heroes—the strong young man and the mighty winged horse.

What Do *You* Think?
Questions for Discussion

࿐

Have you ever been around a toddler who keeps asking the question "Why?" Does your teacher call on you in class with questions from your homework? Do your parents ask you about your day at the dinner table? We are always surrounded by questions that need a specific response. But is it possible to have a question with no right answer?

The following questions are about the book you just read. But this is not a quiz! They are designed to help you look at the people, places, and events from different angles. These questions do not have specific answers. Instead, they might make you think of these stories in a completely new way.

Think carefully about each question and enjoy discovering more about these classic myths.

1. Many of these stories tell of how something came to be. For example, the story "Demeter and Persephone" explains why we have winter. Can you create your own myth to explain how something came to be?

2. Heracles must perform many difficult tasks. What are some of the most difficult ones? Would you be able to complete any of these tasks? Which ones would you never even try?

3. What happens when Pandora opens the box that Zeus and Hera gave her? What did you think of Pandora after she opened the box? Have

you ever been tempted to do something you were told not to?

4. In "Orpheus and Eurydice," Orpheus journeys to the underworld to bring Eurydice back. How is Orpheus able to travel safely into the underworld? What are some of the creatures he confronts? If you were Orpheus, would you have gone down to the underworld to bring back Eurydice?

5. Many of the human characters in the stories have special gifts or talents. What are some of those talents? Which of those would you most like to have? What are your special talents?

6. In "Pygmalion and Galatea," Pygmalion's beautiful statue of a woman becomes a human. If you could sculpt something that would come alive, what would you most want to create?

7. In "Jason and the Golden Fleece," many strangers help Jason complete his challenges. Why do these strangers help Jason? Can you

think of a time when someone helped you do a task? Why did that person help you?

8. If you were Phaeton, would you have asked to drive Apollo's chariot? Can you think of a time when you tried to do something that seemed impossible? How did you feel before you tried? How did you feel after? Did you ever try again?

9. In the story "Pegasus and Bellerophon," the winged horse and the human hero develop a special friendship. Pegasus helps Bellerophon to defeat the Chimera, and they have many more adventures together. Do you have adventures with your pet(s)? What is special about your pet?

10. How do the Greek gods affect what happens to the main characters of the stories? Are they always helpful? In what ways are the gods just like humans?

A Note to Parents and Educators
By *Arthur Pober, EdD*

❧

First impressions are important.

Whether we are meeting new people, going to new places, or picking up a book unknown to us, first impressions can count for a lot. They can lead to warm, lasting memories or can make us shy away from future encounters.

Can you recall your own first impressions and earliest memories of reading the classics?

Do you remember wading through pages and pages of text to prepare for an exam? Or were you the child who hid under the blanket to read with a flashlight, joining forces with Robin Hood to save Maid Marian? Do you remember only how long it took you to read a lengthy novel such as *Little Women*? Or did you become best friends with the March sisters?

Even for a gifted young reader, getting through long chapters with dense language can easily become overwhelming and can obscure the richness of the story and its characters. Reading an abridged, newly crafted version of a classic novel can be the gentle introduction a child needs to explore the characters and story line without the frustrations of difficult vocabulary and complex themes.

Reading an abridged version of a classic novel gives the young reader a sense of independence and the satisfaction of finishing a "grown-up" book. And when a child is engaged with and inspired by a classic story, the tone is set for further exploration of the story's themes, characters, history, and details. As a child's reading skills advance, the desire to tackle the original, unabridged version of the story will naturally emerge.

If made accessible to young readers, these stories can become invaluable tools for understanding themselves in the context of their families and social environments. This is why the Classic Starts series includes questions that stimulate discussion regarding the impact and social relevance of the characters and stories today. These questions can foster lively conversations between children and their parents or teachers. When we look at the issues, values, and standards of past times in terms of how we live now, we can appreciate literature's classic tales in a very personal and engaging way.

Share your love of reading the classics with a young child, and introduce an imaginary world real enough to last a lifetime.

Dr. Arthur Pober, EdD

Dr. Arthur Pober has spent more than twenty years in the fields of early childhood and gifted education. He is the former principal of one of the world's oldest laboratory schools for gifted youngsters, Hunter College Elementary School, and former director of Magnet Schools for the Gifted and Talented for more than twenty-five thousand youngsters in New York City.

Dr. Pober is a recognized authority in the areas of media and child protection and is currently the U.S. representative to the European Institute for the Media and European Advertising Standards Alliance.

Explore these wonderful stories in our
Classic Starts™ library.